AF351533

A Ghostly Wife
and Other Folk-Tales

A Ghostly Wife
and Other Folk-Tales

Lal Behari Dey

Illustrations by
Warwick Goble

HAWK PRESS

Published by

Hawk Press
4836/24, Ansari Road, Daryaganj
New Delhi – 110 002
Phones : 9643330713, +91-11-23278618, +91-11-35676207
E-mail: thehawkpress@gmail.com
www.thehawkpress.com

Copyright © 2023, Editor
ISBN: 978-93-95034-69-2
All rights reserved.

No part of this book may be reproduced, stored in a retrieval
system, transmitted or utilised in any form or by any means,
electronic, mechanical, photocopying, recording or otherwise,
without the prior permission of the copyright owner. Application
for such permission should be addressed to the publisher.

Contents

TO
RICHARD CARNAC TEMPLE
CAPTAIN, BENGAL STAFF CORPS
F.R.G.S., M.R.A.S., M.A.I., ETC.
WHO FIRST SUGGESTED TO THE WRITER
THE IDEA OF COLLECTING
THESE TALES
AND WHO IS DOING SO MUCH
IN THE CAUSE OF INDIAN FOLK-LORE
THIS LITTLE BOOK
IS INSCRIBED

Preface

In my Peasant Life in Bengal I make the peasant boy Govinda spend some hours every evening in listening to stories told by an old woman, who was called Sambhu's mother, and who was the best story-teller in the village. On reading that passage, Captain R. C. Temple, of the Bengal Staff Corps, son of the distinguished Indian administrator Sir Richard Temple, wrote to me to say how interesting it would be to get a collection of those unwritten stories which old women in India recite to little children in the evenings, and to ask whether I could not make such a collection. As I was no stranger to the Mährchen of the Brothers Grimm, to the Norse Tales so admirably told by Dasent, to Arnason's Icelandic Stories translated by Powell, to the Highland Stories done into English by Campbell, and to the fairy stories collected by other writers, and as I believed that the collection suggested would be a contribution, however slight, to that daily increasing literature of folk-lore and comparative mythology which, like comparative philosophy, proves that the swarthy and half-naked peasant on the banks of the Ganges is a cousin, albeit of the hundredth remove, to the fair-skinned and well-dressed Englishman on the banks of the Thames, I readily caught up the idea and cast about for materials. But where was an old story-telling woman to be got? I had myself, when a little boy, heard hundreds—it would be no exaggeration to say thousands—of fairy tales from that same old woman, Sambhu's mother—for she was no fictitious person; she actually lived in the flesh and bore that name; but I had nearly forgotten those stories, at any rate they had all got confused in my head, the tail of one story being joined to the head of another, and the head of a third to the tail of a fourth.

How I wished that poor Sambhu's mother had been alive! But she had gone long, long ago, to that bourne from which no traveller returns, and her son Sambhu, too, had followed her thither. After a great deal of search I found my Gammer Grethel—though not half so old as the Frau Viehmännin of Hesse-Cassel—in the person of a Bengali Christian woman, who, when a little girl and living in her heathen home, had heard many stories from her old grandmother. She was a good story-teller, but her stock was not large; and after I had heard ten from her I had to look about for fresh sources. An old Brahman told me two stories; an old barber, three; an old servant of mine told me two; and the rest I heard from another old Brahman. None of my authorities knew English; they all told the stories in Bengali, and I translated them into English when I came home. I heard many more stories than those contained in the following pages; but I rejected a great many, as they appeared to me to contain spurious additions to the original stories which I had heard when a boy. I have reason to believe that the stories given in this book are a genuine sample of the old old stories told by old Bengali women from age to age through a hundred generations.

Sambhu's mother used always to end every one of her stories—
and every orthodox Bengali story-teller does the same—with
repeating the following formula:—

> *Thus my story endeth,*
> *The Natiya-thorn withereth.*
> *"Why, O Natiya-thorn, dost wither?"*
> *"Why does thy cow on me browse?"*
> *"Why, O cow, dost thou browse?"*
> *"Why does thy neat-herd not tend me?"*
> *"Why, O neat-herd, dost not tend the cow?"*
> *"Why does thy daughter-in-law not give me rice?"*
> *"Why, O daughter-in-law, dost not give rice?"*
> *"Why does my child cry?"*
> *"Why, O child, dost thou cry?"*
> *"Why does the ant bite me?"*
> *"Why, O ant, dost thou bite?"*
> *Koot! koot! koot!*

What these lines mean, why they are repeated at the end of
every story, and what the connection is of the several parts to
one another, I do not know. Perhaps the whole is a string of
nonsense purposely put together to amuse little children.

Lal Behari Day
Hooghly College,
February 27, 1883.

1

The Boy whom
Seven Mothers Suckled

Once upon a time there reigned a king who had seven queens. He was very sad, for the seven queens were all barren. A holy mendicant, however, one day told the king that in a certain forest there grew a tree, on a branch of which hung seven mangoes; if the king himself plucked those mangoes and gave one to each of the queens they would all become mothers. So the king went to the forest, plucked the seven mangoes that grew upon one branch, and gave a mango to each of the queens to eat. In a short time the king's heart was filled with joy, as he heard that the seven queens were all with child.

One day the king was out hunting, when he saw a young lady of peerless beauty cross his path. He fell in love with her, brought her to his palace, and married her. This lady was, however, not a human being, but a Rakshasi; but the king of course did not know it. The king became dotingly fond of her; he did whatever she told him. She said one day to the king, "You say that you love me more than any one else. Let me see whether you really love me so. If you love me, make your seven other queens blind, and let them be killed." The king became very sad at the request of his best-beloved queen, the more so as the seven queens were all with child. But there was nothing for it but to comply with the Rakshasi-queen's request. The eyes of the seven queens were plucked out of their sockets, and the queens themselves were delivered up to the chief minister to be destroyed. But the chief minister was a merciful man. Instead of killing the seven queens he hid them in a cave which was on the side of a hill. In course of time the eldest of the seven queens gave birth to a child. "What shall I do with the child," said she, "now that we are blind and are dying for want of food? Let me kill the child, and let us all eat of its flesh." So saying she killed the infant, and gave to each of her sister-queens a part of the child to eat. The six ate their portion, but the seventh or youngest queen did not eat her share, but laid it beside her. In a few days the second queen also was delivered of a child, and she did with it as her eldest sister had done with hers. So did the third, the fourth, the fifth, and the sixth queen. At last the seventh queen gave birth to a son; but she, instead of following the example of her sister-queens, resolved to nurse the child. The other queens demanded their portions of the newly-born babe. She gave each of them the portion she had got of the six children which had been killed, and which she had not eaten but laid aside. The other queens at once perceived that their portions were dry, and could not therefore be the parts of the child just born. The seventh queen told them that she had made up her mind not to kill the child but to nurse it. The others were glad to hear this, and they all said that they would help her in nursing the child. So the child was suckled by seven mothers, and it became after some years the hardiest and strongest boy that ever lived.

In the meantime the Rakshasi-wife of the king was doing infinite mischief to the royal household and to the capital. What she ate at the royal table did not fill her capacious stomach. She therefore, in the darkness of night, gradually ate up all the members of the royal family, all the king's servants and attendants, all his horses, elephants, and cattle; till none remained in the palace except she herself and her royal consort. After that she used to go out in the evenings into the city and eat up a stray human being here and there. The king was left unattended by servants; there was no person left to cook for him, for no one would take his service. At last the boy who had been suckled by seven mothers, and who had now grown up to a stalwart youth, volunteered his services. He attended on the king, and took every care to prevent the queen from swallowing him up, for he went away home long before nightfall; and the Rakshasi-queen never seized her victims except at night. Hence the queen determined in some other way to get rid of the boy. As the boy always boasted that he was equal to any work, however hard, the queen told him that she was suffering from some disease which could be cured only by eating a certain species of melon, which was twelve cubits long, but the stone of which was thirteen cubits long, and that that fruit could be had only from her mother, who lived on the other side of the ocean. She gave him a letter of introduction to her mother, in which she requested her to devour the boy the moment he put the letter into her hands. The boy, suspecting foul play, tore up the letter and proceeded on his journey. The dauntless youth passed through many lands, and at last stood on the shore of the ocean, on the other side of which was the country of the Rakshasis. He then bawled as loud as he could, and said, "Granny! granny! come and save your daughter; she is dangerously ill." An old Rakshasi on the other side of the ocean heard the words, crossed the ocean, came to the boy, and on hearing the message took the boy on her back and re-crossed the ocean. So the boy was in the country of the Rakshasis. The twelve-cubit melon with its thirteen-cubit stone was given to the boy at once, and he was told to perform the journey back. But the boy pleaded fatigue, and begged to be allowed to rest one day. To this the old Rakshasi consented. Observing a stout club and a rope hanging in the Rakshasi's room, the boy inquired what they were there for. She replied, "Child, by that club and rope I cross the ocean. If any one takes the club and the rope in his hands, and addresses them in the following magical words—

> *"O stout club! O strong rope!*
> *Take me at once to the other side,"*

then immediately the club and rope will take him to the other side of the ocean." Observing a bird in a cage hanging in one corner of the room, the boy inquired what it was. The old Rakshasi replied, "It contains a secret, child, which must not be disclosed to mortals, and yet how can I hide it from my own grandchild? That bird, child, contains the life of your mother. If the bird is killed, your mother will at once die." Armed with these secrets, the boy went to bed that night. Next morning the old Rakshasi, together with all the other Rakshasis, went to distant countries for forage. The boy took down the cage from the ceiling, as well as the club and rope. Having well secured the bird, he addressed the club and rope thus—

"*O stout club! O strong rope!*
Take me at once to the other side."

In the twinkling of an eye the boy was put on this side of the ocean. He then retraced his steps, came to the queen, and gave her, to her astonishment, the twelve-cubit melon with its thirteen-cubit stone; but the cage with the bird in it he kept carefully concealed.

"*A monstrous bird comes out apparently from the palace*"

In the course of time the people of the city came to the king and said, "A monstrous bird comes out apparently from the palace every evening, and seizes the passengers in the streets and swallows them up. This has been going on for so long a time that the city has become almost desolate." The king could not make out what this monstrous bird was. The king's servant, the boy, replied that he knew the monstrous bird, and that he would kill it provided the queen stood beside the king. By royal command the queen was made to stand beside the king. The boy then took the bird from the cage which he had brought from the other side of the ocean, on seeing which she fell into a fainting fit. Turning to the king the boy said, "Sire, you will soon perceive who the monstrous bird is that devours your subjects every evening. As I tear off each limb of this bird, the corresponding limb of the man-devourer will fall off." The boy then tore off one leg of the bird in his hand; immediately, to the astonishment of the whole assembly, for the citizens were all present, one of the legs of the queen fell off. And when the boy squeezed the throat of the bird, the queen gave up the ghost. The boy then related his own history and that of his mother and his stepmothers. The seven queens, whose eyesight was miraculously restored, were brought back to the palace; and the boy that was suckled by seven mothers was recognised by the king as his rightful heir. So they lived together happily.

2

The Story of Prince Sobur

Once a time there lived a certain merchant who had seven daughters. One day the merchant put to his daughters the question: "By whose fortune do you get your living?" The eldest daughter answered—"Papa, I get my living by your fortune." The same answer was given by the second daughter, the third, the fourth, the fifth, and the sixth; but his youngest daughter said—"I get my living by my own fortune." The merchant got very angry with the youngest daughter, and said to her—"As you are so ungrateful as to say that you get your living by your own fortune, let me see how you fare alone. This very day you shall leave my house without a pice in your pocket." He forthwith called his palki-bearers, and ordered them to take away the girl and leave her in the midst of a forest. The girl begged hard to be allowed to take with her her work-box containing her needles and threads. She was allowed to do so. She then got into the palki, which the bearers lifted on their shoulders. The bearers had not gone many hundred yards to the tune of "Hoon! hoon! hoon! hoon! hoon! hoon!" when an old woman bawled out to them and bid them stop. On coming up to the palki, she said, "Where are you taking away my daughter?" for she was the nurse of the merchant's youngest child. The bearers replied, "The merchant has ordered us to take her away and leave her in the midst of a forest; and we are going to do his bidding." "I must go with her," said the old woman. "How will you be able to keep pace with us, as we must needs run?" said the bearers. "Anyhow I must go where my daughter goes," rejoined the old woman. The upshot was that, at the entreaty of the merchant's youngest daughter, the old woman was put inside the palki along with her. In the afternoon the palki-bearers reached a dense forest. They went far into it; and towards sunset they put down the girl and the old woman at the foot of a large tree, and retraced their steps homewards.

The case of the merchant's youngest daughter was truly pitiable. She was scarcely fourteen years old; she had been bred in the lap of luxury; and she was now here at sundown in the heart of what seemed an interminable forest, with not a penny in her pocket, and with no other protection than what could be given her by an old, decrepit, imbecile woman. The very trees of the forest looked upon her with pity. The gigantic tree, at whose foot she was mingling her tears with those of the old woman, said to her (for trees could speak in those days)—"Unhappy girl! I much pity you. In a short time the wild beasts of the forest will come out of their lairs and roam about for their prey; and they are sure to devour you and your companion. But I can help you; I will make an opening for you in my trunk. When you see the opening go into it; I will then close it up; and you will remain safe inside; nor can the wild beasts touch you." In a moment the trunk of the tree was split into two. The merchant's daughter and the old woman went inside the hollow, on which the tree resumed its natural shape. When the shades of night darkened the forest the wild beasts came out of their lairs. The fierce tiger was there; the wild bear was there; the hard-skinned rhinoceros was there; the bushy bear was there; the musty elephant was there; and the horned buffalo was there. They all growled round about the tree, for they got the scent of human blood. The merchant's daughter and the old woman heard from within the tree the growl of the beasts. The beasts came dashing against the tree; they broke its branches; they pierced its trunk with their horns; they scratched its bark with their claws: but in vain. The merchant's daughter and her old nurse were safe within. Towards dawn the wild beasts went away. After sunrise the good tree said to her two inmates, "Unhappy women, the wild beasts have gone into their lairs after greatly tormenting me. The sun is up; you can now come out." So saying the tree split itself into two, and the merchant's daughter and the old woman came out. They saw the extent of the mischief done by the wild beasts to the tree. Many of its branches had been broken down; in many places the trunk had been pierced; and in other places the bark had been stripped off. The merchant's daughter said to the tree, "Good mother, you are truly good to give us shelter at such a fearful cost. You must be in great pain from the torture to which the wild beasts subjected you last night." So saying she went to the tank which was near the tree, and bringing thence a quantity of mud, she besmeared the trunk with it, especially those parts which had been pierced and scratched. After she had done this, the tree said, "Thank you, my good girl, I am now greatly relieved of my pain. I am, however, concerned not so much about myself as about you both. You must be hungry, not having eaten the whole of yesterday. And what can I give you? I have no fruit of my own to give you. Give to the old woman whatever money you have, and let her go into the city hard by and buy some food." They said they had no money. On searching, however, in the work-box she found five cowries.[1] The tree then told the old woman to go with the cowries to the city and buy some khai.[2] The old woman went to the city, which was not far, and said to one confectioner, "Please give me five cowries' worth of khai." The confectioner laughed at her and said, "Be off, you old hag, do you think khai can be had for five cowries?" She tried another shop, and the shopkeeper, thinking the woman to be in great distress, compassionately gave her a large quantity of khai for the five cowries.

"Hundreds of peacocks of gorgeous plumes came to the embankments to eat the khai"

When the old woman returned with the khai, the tree said to the merchant's daughter, "Each of you eat a little of the khai, lay by more than half, and strew the rest on the embankments of the tank all round." They did as they were bidden, though they did not understand the reason why they were told to scatter the khai on the sides of the tank. They spent the day in bewailing their fate, and at night they were housed inside the trunk of the tree as on the previous night. The wild beasts came as before, further mutilated the tree, and tortured it as in the preceding night. But during the night a scene was being enacted on the embankments of the tank of which the two women saw the outcome only on the following morning. Hundreds of peacocks of gorgeous plumes came to the embankments to eat the khai which had been strewed on them; and as they strove with each other for the tempting food many of their plumes fell off their bodies. Early in the morning the tree told the two women to gather the plumes together, out of which the merchant's daughter made a beautiful fan. This fan was taken into the city to the palace, where the son of the king admired it greatly and paid for it a large sum of money. As each morning a quantity of plumes was collected, every day one fan was made and sold. So that in a short time the two women got rich. The tree then advised them to employ men in building a house for them to live in. Accordingly bricks were burnt, trees were cut down for beams and rafters, bricks were reduced to powder, lime was manufactured, and in a few months a stately, palace-like house was built for the merchant's daughter and her old nurse. It was thought advisable to lay out the adjoining grounds as a garden, and to dig a tank for supplying them with water.

In the meantime the merchant himself with his wife and six

daughters had been frowned upon by the goddess of wealth. By a sudden stroke of misfortune he lost all his money, his house and property were sold, and he, his wife, and six daughters, were turned adrift penniless into the world. It so happened that they lived in a village not far from the place where the two strange women had built a palace and were digging a tank. As the once rich merchant was now supporting his family by the pittance which he obtained every day for his manual labour, he bethought himself of employing himself as a day labourer in digging the tank of the strange lady on the skirts of the forest. His wife said she would also go to dig the tank with him. So one day while the strange lady was amusing herself from the window of her palace with looking at the labourers digging her tank, to her utter surprise she saw her father and mother coming towards the palace, apparently to engage themselves as day labourers. Tears ran down her cheeks as she looked at them, for they were clothed in rags. She immediately sent servants to bring them inside the house. The poor man and woman were frightened beyond measure. They saw that the tank was all ready; and as it was customary in those days to offer a human sacrifice when the digging was over, they thought that they were called inside in order to be sacrificed. Their fears increased when they were told to throw away their rags and to put on fine clothes which were given to them. The strange lady of the palace, however, soon dispelled their fears; for she told them that she was their daughter, fell on their necks and wept. The rich daughter related her adventures, and the father felt she was right when she said that she lived upon her own fortune and not on that of her father. She gave her father a large fortune, which enabled him to go to the city in which he formerly lived, and to set himself up again as a merchant.

The merchant now bethought himself of going in his ship to distant countries for purposes of trade. All was ready. He got on board, ready to start, but, strange to say, the ship would not move. The merchant was at a loss what to make of this. At last the idea occurred to him that he had asked each of his six daughters, who were living with him, what thing she wished he should bring for her; but he had not asked that question of his seventh daughter who had made him rich. He therefore immediately despatched a messenger to his youngest daughter, asking her what she wished her father to bring for her on his return from his mercantile travels. When the messenger arrived she was engaged in her devotions, and hearing that a messenger had arrived from her father she said to him "Sobur," meaning "wait." The messenger understood that she wanted her father to bring for her something called Sobur. He returned to the merchant and told him that she wanted him to bring for her Sobur. The ship now moved of itself, and the merchant started on his travels. He visited many ports, and by selling his goods obtained immense profit. The things his six daughters wanted him to bring for them he easily got, but Sobur, the thing which he understood his youngest daughter wished to have, he could get nowhere. He asked at every port whether Sobur could be had there, but the merchants all told him that they had never heard of such an article of commerce. At the last port he went through the streets bawling out—"Wanted Sobur! wanted Sobur!" The cry attracted the notice of the son of the king of that country whose name was Sobur. The prince, hearing from the merchant that his daughter wanted Sobur, said that he had the article in question, and bringing out a small box of wood containing a magical fan with a looking-glass in it, said—"This is Sobur which your daughter wishes to have." The merchant having obtained the long-wished-for Sobur weighed anchor, and sailed for his native land. On his arrival he sent to his youngest daughter the said wonderful box. The daughter, thinking it to be a common wooden box, laid it aside. Some days after when she was at leisure she bethought herself of opening the box which her father had sent her. When she opened it she saw in it a beautiful fan, and in it a looking-glass. As she shook the fan, in a moment the Prince Sobur stood before her, and said—"You called me, here I am. What's your wish?" The merchant's daughter, astonished at the sudden appearance of a prince of such exquisite beauty, asked who he was, and how he had made his appearance there. The prince told her of the circumstances under which he gave the box to her father, and informed her of the secret that whenever the fan would be shaken he would make his appearance. The prince lived for a day or two in the house of the merchant's daughter, who entertained him hospitably. The upshot was, that they fell in love with each other, and vowed to each other to be husband and wife. The prince returned to his royal father and told him that he had selected a wife for himself. The day for the wedding was fixed. The merchant and his six daughters were invited. The nuptial knot was tied. But there was death in the marriage-bed. The six daughters of the merchant, envying the happy lot of their youngest sister, had determined to put an end to the life of her newly-wedded husband. They broke several bottles, reduced the broken pieces into fine powder, and scattered it profusely on the bed. The prince, suspecting no danger, laid himself down in the bed; but he had scarcely been there two minutes when he felt acute pain through his whole system, for the fine bottle-powder had gone through every pore of his body. As the prince became restless through pain, and was shrieking aloud, his attendants hastily took him away to his own country.

The king and queen, the parents of Prince Sobur, consulted all the physicians and surgeons of the kingdom; but in vain. The young prince was day and night screaming with pain, and no one could ascertain the disease, far less give him relief. The grief of the merchant's daughter may be imagined. The marriage knot had been scarcely tied when her husband was attacked, as she thought, by a terrible disease and carried away many hundreds of miles off. Though she had never seen her husband's country she determined to go there and nurse him. She put on the garb of a Sannyasi, and with a dagger in her hand set out on her journey. Of tender years, and unaccustomed to make long journeys on foot, she soon got weary and sat under a tree to rest. On the top of the tree was the nest of the divine bird Bihangama and his mate Bihangami. They were not in their nest at the time, but two of their young ones were in it. Suddenly the young ones on the top of the tree gave a scream which roused the half-drowsy merchant's daughter whom we shall now call the young Sannyasi. He saw near him a huge serpent raising its hood and about to climb into the tree. In a moment he cut the serpent into two, on which the young birds left off screaming. Shortly after the Bihangama and Bihangami came sailing through the air; and the latter said to the former—"I suppose our offspring as usual have been devoured by our great enemy the serpent. Ah me! I do not hear the cries of my young ones." On nearing the nest, however, they were agreeably surprised to find their offspring alive. The young ones told their dams how the young Sannyasi under the tree had destroyed the serpent. And sure enough the snake was lying there cut into two.

The Bihangami then said to her mate—"The young Sannyasi has saved our offspring from death, I wish we could do him some service in return." The Bihangama replied, "We shall presently do her service, for the person under the tree is not a man but a woman. She got married only last night to Prince Sobur, who, a few hours after, when jumping into his bed, had every pore of his body pierced with fine particles of ground bottles which had been spread over his bed by his envious sisters-in-law. He is still suffering pain in his native land, and, indeed, is at the point of death. And his heroic bride taking the garb of a Sannyasi is going to nurse him." "But," asked the Bihangami, "is there no cure for the prince?" "Yes, there is," replied the Bihangama: "if our dung which is lying on the ground round about, and which is hardened, be reduced to powder, and applied by means of a brush to the body of the prince after bathing him seven times with seven jars of water and seven jars of milk, Prince Sobur will undoubtedly get well." "But," asked the Bihangami, "how can the poor daughter of the merchant walk such a distance? It must take her many days, by which time the poor prince will have died." "I can," replied the Bihangama, "take the young lady on my back, and put her in the capital of Prince Sobur, and bring her back, provided she does not take any presents there." The merchant's daughter, in the garb of a Sannyasi, heard this conversation between the two birds, and begged the Bihangama to take her on his back. To this the bird readily consented. Before mounting on her aerial car she gathered a quantity of birds' dung and reduced it to fine powder. Armed with this potent drug she got up on the back of the kind bird, and sailing through the air with the rapidity of lightning, soon reached the capital of Prince Sobur. The young Sannyasi went up to the gate of the palace, and sent word to the king that he was acquainted with potent drugs and would cure the prince in a few hours. The king, who had tried all the best doctors in the kingdom without success, looked upon the Sannyasi as a mere pretender, but on the advice of his councillors agreed to give him a trial. The Sannyasi ordered seven jars of water and seven jars of milk to be brought to him. He poured the contents of all the jars on the body of the prince. He then applied, by means of a feather, the dung-powder he had already prepared to every pore of the prince's body. Thereafter seven jars of water and seven jars of milk were again six times poured upon him. When the prince's body was wiped, he felt perfectly well. The king ordered that the richest treasures he had should be presented to the wonderful doctor; but the Sannyasi refused to take any. He only wanted a ring from the prince's finger to preserve as a memorial. The ring was readily given him. The merchant's daughter hastened to the sea-shore where the Bihangama was awaiting her. In a moment they reached the tree of the divine birds. Hence the young bride walked to her house on the skirts of the forest. The following day she shook the magical fan, and forthwith Prince Sobur appeared before her. When the lady showed him the ring, he learnt with infinite surprise that his own wife was the doctor that cured him. The prince took away his bride to his palace in his far-off kingdom, forgave his sisters-in-law, lived happily for scores of years, and was blessed with children, grandchildren, and great-grandchildren.

1. Shells used as money, one hundred and sixty of which could have been got a few years ago for one pice.

2. Fried paddy.

3

The Origin of Opium[1]

Once upon a time there lived on the banks of the holy Ganga a Rishi,[2] who spent his days and nights in the performance of religious rites and in meditation upon God. From sunrise to sunset he sat on the river bank engaged in devotion, and at night he took shelter in a hut of palm-leaves which his own hand had raised in a bush hard by. There were no men and women for miles round. In the hut, however, there was a mouse, which used to live upon the leavings of the Rishi's supper. As it was not in the nature of the sage to hurt any living thing, our mouse never ran away from him, but, on the contrary, went to him, touched his feet, and played with him. The Rishi, partly in kindness to the little brute, and partly to have some one by to talk to at times, gave the mouse the power of speech. One night the mouse, standing on its hind-legs and joining together its fore-legs reverently, said to the Rishi, "Holy sage, you have been so kind as to give me the power to speak like men. If it will not displease your reverence, I have one more boon to ask." "What is it?" said the Rishi. "What is it, little mousie? Say what you want." The mouse answered—"When your reverence goes in the day to the river-side for devotion, a cat comes to the hut to catch me. And had it not been for fear of your reverence, the cat would have eaten me up long ago; and I fear it will eat me some day. My prayer is that I may be changed into a cat that I may prove a match for my foe." The Rishi became propitious to the mouse, and threw some holy water on its body, and it was at once changed into a cat.

Some nights after, the Rishi asked his pet, "Well, little puss, how do you like your present life?" "Not much, your reverence," answered the cat. "Why not?" demanded the sage. "Are you not strong enough to hold your own against all the cats in the world?" "Yes," rejoined the cat. "Your reverence has made me a strong cat, able to cope with all the cats in the world. But I do not now fear cats; I have got a new foe. Whenever your reverence goes to the river-side, a pack of dogs comes to the hut, and sets up such a loud barking that I am frightened out of my life. If your reverence will not be displeased with me, I beg you to change me into a dog." The Rishi said, "Be turned into a dog," and the cat forthwith became a dog.

Some days passed, when one night the dog said thus to the Rishi: "I cannot thank your reverence enough for your kindness to me. I was but a poor mouse, and you not only gave me speech but turned me into a cat; and again you were kind enough to change me into a dog. As a dog, however, I suffer a great deal of trouble, I do not get enough food: my only food is the leavings of your supper, but that is not sufficient to fill the maw of such a large beast as you have made me. O how I envy those apes who jump about from tree to tree, and eat all sorts of delicious fruits! If your reverence will not get angry with me, I pray that I be changed into an ape." The kind-hearted sage readily granted his pet's wish, and the dog became an ape.

Our ape was at first wild with joy. He leaped from one tree to another, and sucked every luscious fruit he could find. But his joy was short-lived. Summer came on with its drought. As a monkey he found it hard to drink water out of a river or of a pool; and he saw the wild boars splashing in the water all the day long. He envied their lot, and exclaimed, "O how happy those boars are! All day their bodies are cooled and refreshed by water. I wish I were a boar." Accordingly at night he recounted to the Rishi the troubles of the life of an ape and the pleasures of that of a boar, and begged of him to change him into a boar. The sage, whose kindness knew no bounds, complied with his pet's request, and turned him into a wild boar. For two whole days our boar kept his body soaking wet, and on the third day, as he was splashing about in his favourite element, whom should he see but the king of the country riding on a richly caparisoned elephant. The king was out hunting, and it was only by a lucky chance that our boar escaped being bagged. He dwelt in his own mind on the dangers attending the life of a wild boar, and envied the lot of the stately elephant who was so fortunate as to carry about the king of the country on his back. He longed to be an elephant, and at night besought the Rishi to make him one.

Our elephant was roaming about in the wilderness, when he saw the king out hunting. The elephant went towards the king's suite with the view of being caught. The king, seeing the elephant at a distance, admired it on account of its beauty, and gave orders that it should be caught and tamed. Our elephant was easily caught, and taken into the royal stables, and was soon tamed. It so chanced that the queen expressed a wish to bathe in the waters of the holy Ganga. The king, who wished to accompany his royal consort, ordered that the newly-caught elephant should be brought to him. The king and queen mounted on his back. One would suppose that the elephant had now got his wishes, as the king had mounted on his back. But no. There was a fly in the ointment. The elephant, who looked upon himself as a lordly beast, could not brook the idea that a woman, though a queen, should ride on his back. He thought himself degraded. He jumped up so violently that both the king and queen fell to the ground. The king carefully picked up the queen, took her in his arms, asked her whether she had been much hurt, wiped off the dust from her clothes with his handkerchief, and tenderly kissed her a hundred times. Our elephant, after witnessing the king's caresses, scampered off to the woods as fast as his legs could carry him. As he ran he thought within himself thus: "After all, I see that a queen is the happiest of all creatures. Of what infinite regard is she the object! The king lifted her up, took her in his arms, made many tender inquiries, wiped off the dust from her clothes with his own royal hands, and kissed her a hundred times! O the happiness of being a queen! I must tell the Rishi to make me a queen!" So saying the elephant, after traversing the woods, went at sunset to the Rishi's hut, and fell prostrate on the ground at the feet of the holy sage. The Rishi said, "Well, what's the news? Why have you left the king's stud?" "What shall I say to your reverence? You have been very kind to me; you have granted every wish of mine. I have one more boon to ask, and it will be the last. By becoming an elephant I have got only my bulk increased, but not my happiness. I see that of all creatures a queen is the happiest in the world. Do, holy father, make me a queen." "Silly child," answered the Rishi, "how can I make you a queen? Where can I get a kingdom for you, and a royal husband to boot? All I can do is to change you into an exquisitely beautiful girl, possessed of charms to captivate the heart of a prince, if ever the gods grant you an interview with some great prince! "Our elephant agreed to the change; and in a moment the sagacious beast was transformed into a beautiful young lady, to whom the holy sage gave the name of Postomani, or the poppy-seed lady.

Postomani lived in the Rishi's hut, and spent her time in tending the flowers and watering the plants. One day, as she was sitting at the door of the hut during the Rishi's absence, she saw a man dressed in a very rich garb come towards the cottage. She stood up and asked the stranger who he was, and what he had come there for. The stranger answered that he had come a-hunting in those parts, that he had been chasing in vain a deer, that he felt thirsty, and that he came to the hut of the hermit for refreshment.

Postomani. Stranger, look upon this cot as your own house. I'll do everything I can to make you comfortable; I am only sorry we are too poor suitably to entertain, a man of your rank, for if I mistake not you are the king of this country.

The king smiled. Postomani then brought out a water-pot, and made as if she would wash the feet of her royal guest with her own hands, when the king said, "Holy maid, do not touch my feet, for I am only a Kshatriya, and you are the daughter of a holy sage."

Postomani. Noble sir, I am not the daughter of the Rishi, neither am I a Brahmani girl; so there can be no harm in my touching your feet. Besides, you are my guest, and I am bound to wash your feet.

King. Forgive my impertinence. What caste do you belong to?

Postomani. I have heard from the sage that my parents were Kshatriyas.

King. May I ask you whether your father was a king, for your uncommon beauty and your stately demeanour show that you are a born princess.

"'You would adorn the palace of the mightiest sovereign'"

Postomani, without answering the question, went inside the hut, brought out a tray of the most delicious fruits, and set it before the king. The king, however, would not touch the fruits till the maid had answered his questions. When pressed hard Postomani gave the following answer: "The holy sage says that my father was a king. Having been overcome in battle, he, along with my mother, fled into the woods. My poor father was eaten up by a tiger, and my mother at that time was brought to bed of me, and she closed her eyes as I opened mine. Strange to say, there was a bee-hive on the tree at the foot of which I lay; drops of honey fell into my mouth and kept alive the spark of life till the kind Rishi found me and brought me into his hut. This is the simple story of the wretched girl who now stands before the king."

King. Call not yourself wretched. You are the loveliest and most beautiful of women. You would adorn the palace of the mightiest sovereign.

The upshot was, that the king made love to the girl and they were joined in marriage by the Rishi. Postomani was treated as the favourite queen, and the former queen was in disgrace. Postomani's happiness, however, was short-lived. One day as she was standing by a well, she became giddy, fell into the water, and died. The Rishi then appeared before the king and said: "O king, grieve not over the past. What is fixed by fate must come to pass. The queen, who has just been drowned, was not of royal blood. She was born a mouse; I then changed her successively, according to her own wish, into a cat, a dog, an ape, a boar, an elephant, and a beautiful girl. Now that she is gone, do you again take into favour your former queen. As for my reputed daughter, through the favour of the gods I'll make her name immortal. Let her body remain in the well; fill the well up with earth. Out of her flesh and bones will grow a tree which shall be called after her Posto, that is, the Poppy tree. From this tree will be obtained a drug called opium, which will be celebrated as a powerful medicine through all ages, and which will always be either swallowed or smoked as a wonderful narcotic to the end of time. The opium swallower or smoker will have one quality of each of the animals to which Postomani was transformed. He will be mischievous like a mouse, fond of milk like a cat, quarrelsome like a dog, filthy like an ape, savage like a boar, and high-tempered like a queen."

1. This story is not my own. It was recited to me by a story-teller of the other sex who rejoices in the nom de plume "An Inmate of the Calcutta Lunatic Asylum."
2. A holy sage.

4

Strike but Hear

nce upon a time there reigned a king who had three sons. His subjects one day came to him and said, "O incarnation of justice! the kingdom is infested with thieves and robbers. Our property is not safe. We pray your majesty to catch hold of these thieves and punish them." The king said to his sons, "O my sons, I am old, but you are all in the prime of manhood. How is it that my kingdom is full of thieves? I look to you to catch hold of these thieves." The three princes then made up their minds to patrol the city every night. With this view they set up a station in the outskirts of the city, where they kept their horses. In the early part of the night the eldest prince rode upon his horse and went through the whole city, but did not see a single thief. He came back to the station. About midnight the second prince got upon his horse and rode through every part of the city, but he did not see or hear of a single thief. He came also back to the station. Some hours after midnight the youngest prince went the rounds, and when he came near the gate of the palace where his father lived, he saw a beautiful woman coming out of the palace. The prince accosted the woman, and asked who she was and where she was going at that hour of the night. The woman answered, "I am Rajlakshmi,[1] the guardian deity of this palace. The king will be killed this night. I am therefore not needed here. I am going away." The prince did not know what to make of this message. After a moment's reflection he said to the goddess, "But suppose the king is not killed to-night, then have you any objection to return to the palace and stay there?" "I have no objection," replied the goddess. The prince then begged the goddess to go in, promising to do his best to prevent the king from being killed. Then the goddess entered the palace again, and in a moment went the prince knew not whither.

The prince went straight into the bedroom of his royal father. There he lay immersed in deep sleep. His second and young wife, the stepmother of our prince, was sleeping in another bed in the room. A light was burning dimly. What was his surprise when the prince saw a huge cobra going round and round the golden bedstead on which his father was sleeping. The prince with his sword cut the serpent in two. Not satisfied with killing the cobra, he cut it up into a hundred pieces, and put them inside the pan dish[2] which was in the room. While the prince was cutting up the serpent a drop of blood fell on the breast of his stepmother who was sleeping hard by. The prince was in great distress.

"He saw a beautiful woman coming out of the palace"

He said to himself, "I have saved my father but killed my mother." How was the drop of blood to be taken out of his mother's breast? He wrapped round his tongue a piece of cloth sevenfold, and with it licked up the drop of blood. But while he was in the act of doing this, his stepmother woke up, and opening her eyes saw that it was her stepson, the youngest prince. The young prince rushed out of the room. The queen, intending to ruin the youngest prince, whom she hated, called out to her husband, "My lord, my lord, are you awake? are you awake? Rouse yourself up. Here is a nice piece of business." The king on awaking inquired what the matter was. "The matter, my lord? Your worthy son, the youngest prince, of whom you speak so highly, was just here. I caught him in the act of touching my breast. Doubtless he came with a wicked intent. And this is your worthy son!" The king was horror-struck. The prince went to the station to his brothers, but told them nothing.

Early in the morning the king called his eldest son to him and said, "If a man to whom I intrust my honour and my life prove faithless, how should he be punished?" The eldest prince replied, "Doubtless such a man's head should be cut off; but before you kill, you should see whether the man is really faithless." "What do you mean?" inquired the king. "Let your majesty be pleased to listen," answered the prince.

"Once on a time there lived a goldsmith who had a grown-up son. And this son had a wife who had the rare faculty of understanding the language of beasts; but neither her husband nor any one else knew that she had this uncommon gift. One night she was lying in bed beside her husband in their house, which was close to a river, when she heard a jackal howl out, 'There goes a carcase floating on the river; is there any one who will take off the diamond ring from the finger of the dead man and give me the corpse to eat?' The woman understood the jackal's language, got up from bed and went to the river-side. The husband, who was not asleep, followed his wife at some distance so as not to be observed by her. The woman went into the water, tugged the floating corpse towards the shore, and saw the diamond ring on the finger. Unable to loosen it with her hand, as the fingers of the dead body had swelled, she bit it off with her teeth, and put the dead body upon land. She then went to her bed, whither she had been preceded by her husband. The young goldsmith lay beside his wife almost petrified with fear, for he concluded after what he saw that his wife was not a human being but a Rakshasi. He spent the rest of the night in tossing in his bed, and early in the morning spoke to his father in the following manner: 'Father, the woman whom thou hast given me to wife is not a real woman but a Rakshasi. Last night as I was lying in bed with her, I heard outside the house, towards the river-side, a jackal set up a fearful howl. On this she, thinking that I was asleep, got up from bed, opened the door, and went out to the river-side. Surprised to see her go out alone at the dead hour of night, I suspected evil and followed her, but so that she could not see me. What did she do, do you think? O horror of horrors! She went into the stream, dragged towards the shore the dead body of a man which was floating by, and began to eat it! I saw this with mine own eyes. I then returned home while she was feasting upon the carcase, and jumped into bed. In a few minutes she also returned, bolted the door, and lay beside me. O my father, how can I live with a Rakshasi? She will certainly kill me and eat me up one night.' The old goldsmith was not a little shocked to hear this account. Both father and son agreed that the woman should be taken into the forest and there left to be devoured by wild beasts. Accordingly the young goldsmith spoke to his wife thus: 'My dear love, you had better not cook much this morning; only boil rice and burn a brinjal, for I must take you to-day to see your father and mother, who are dying to see you.' At the mention of her father's house she became full of joy, and finished the cooking in no time. The husband and wife snatched a hasty breakfast and started on their journey. The way lay through a dense jungle, in which the goldsmith bethought himself of leaving his wife alone to be eaten up by wild beasts. But while they were passing through this jungle the woman heard a serpent hiss, the meaning of which hissing, as understood by her, was as follows: 'O passer-by, how thankful should I be to you if you would catch hold of that croaking frog in yonder hole, which is full of gold and precious stones, and give me the frog to swallow, and you take the gold and precious stones.' The woman forthwith made for the frog, and began digging the hole with a stick. The young goldsmith was now quaking with fear, thinking his Rakshasi-wife was about to kill him. She called out to him and said, 'Husband, take up all this large quantity of gold and these precious stones.' The goldsmith, not knowing what to make of it, timidly went to the place, and to his infinite surprise saw the gold and the precious stones. They took up as much as they could. On the husband's asking his wife how she came to know of the existence of all this riches, she said that she understood the language of animals, and that the snake coiled up hard by had informed her of it. The goldsmith, on finding out what an accomplished wife he was blessed with, said to her, 'My love, it has got very late to-day; it would be impossible to reach your father's house before nightfall, and we may be devoured by wild beasts in the jungle; I propose therefore that we both return home.' It took them a long time to reach home, for they were laden with a large quantity of gold and precious stones. On coming near the house, the goldsmith said to his wife, 'My dear, you go by the back door, while I go by the front door and see my father in his shop and show him all this gold and these precious stones.' So she entered the house by the back door, and the moment she entered she was met by the old goldsmith, who had come that minute into the house for some purpose with a hammer in his hand. The old goldsmith, when he saw his Rakshasi daughter-in-law, concluded in his mind that she had killed and swallowed up his son. He therefore struck her on the head with the hammer, and she immediately died. That moment the son came into the house, but it was too late. Hence it is that I told your majesty that before you cut off a man's head you should inquire whether the man is really guilty."

*"'Husband, take up all this large quantity of gold and
these precious stones'"*

The king then called his second son to him, and said, "If a
man to whom I intrust my honour and my life prove faithless,
how should he be punished?" The second prince replied,
"Doubtless such a man's head should be cut off, but before
you kill you should see whether the man is really faithless."

"What do you mean?" inquired the king. "Let your majesty be pleased to listen," answered the prince.

"Once on a time there reigned a king who was very fond of going out a-hunting. Once while he was out hunting his horse took him into a dense forest far from his followers. He rode on and on, and did not see either villages or towns. He became very thirsty, but he could see neither pond, lake, nor stream. At last he found something dripping from the top of a tree. Concluding it to be rain-water which had rested in some cavity of the tree, he stood on horseback under the tree and caught the dripping contents in a small cup. It was, however, no rain-water. A huge cobra, which was on the top of the tree, was dashing in rage its fangs against the tree; and its poison was coming out and was falling in drops. The king, however, thought it was rain-water; though his horse knew better. When the cup was nearly filled with the liquid snake-poison, and the king was about to drink it off, the horse, to save the life of his royal master, so moved about that the cup fell from the king's hand and all the liquid spilled about. The king became very angry with his horse, and with his sword gave a cut to the horse's neck, and the horse died immediately. Hence it is that I told your majesty that before you cut off a man's head you should inquire whether the man is really guilty."

The king then called to him his third and youngest son, and said, "If a man to whom I intrust my honour and my life prove faithless, how should he be punished?" The youngest prince replied, "Doubtless such a man's head should be cut off, but before you kill you should see whether the man is really faithless." "What do you mean?" inquired the king. "Let your majesty be pleased to listen," answered the prince.

"Once on a time there reigned a king who had in his palace a remarkable bird of the Suka species. One day as the Suka went out to the fields for an airing, he saw his dad and dam, who pressed him to come and spend some days with them in their nest in some far-off land. The Suka answered he would be very happy to come, but he could not go without the king's leave; he added that he would speak to the king that very day, and would be ready to go the following morning if his dad and dam would come to that very spot. The Suka spoke to the king, and the king gave leave with reluctance as he was very fond of the bird. So the next morning the Suka met his dad and dam at the place appointed, and went with them to his paternal nest on the top of some high tree in a far-off land. The three birds lived happily together for a fortnight, at the end of which period the Suka said to his dad and dam, 'My beloved parents, the king granted me leave only for a fortnight, and to-day the fortnight is over: to-morrow I must start for the city of the king.' His dad and dam readily agreed to the reasonable proposal, and told him to take a present to the king. After laying their heads together for some time they agreed that the present should be a fruit of the tree of Immortality. So early next morning the Suka plucked a fruit off the tree of Immortality, and carefully catching it in his beak, started on his aerial journey. As he had a heavy weight to carry, the Suka was not able to reach the city of the king that day, and was benighted on the road. He took shelter in a tree, and was at a loss to know where to keep the fruit. If he kept it in his beak it was sure, he thought, to fall out when he fell asleep. Fortunately he saw a hole in the trunk of the tree in which he had taken shelter, and accordingly put the fruit in it. It so happened that in that hole there was a snake; in the course of the night the snake darted its fangs on the fruit, and thus besmeared it with its poison. Early before crow-cawing the Suka, suspecting nothing, took up the fruit of Immortality in its beak, and began his aerial voyage. The Suka reached the palace while the king was sitting with his ministers. The king was delighted to see his pet bird come again, and greatly admired the beautiful fruit which the Suka had brought as a present. The fruit was very fair to look at; it was the loveliest fruit in all the earth; and as its name implies it makes the eater of it immortal. The king was going to eat it, but his courtiers said that it was not advisable for the king to eat it, as it might be a poisonous fruit. He accordingly threw it to a crow which was perched on the wall; the crow ate a part of it; but in a moment the crow fell down and died. The king, imagining that the Suka had intended to take away his life, took hold of the bird and killed it. The king ordered the stone of the deadly fruit, as it was thought to be, to be planted in a garden outside the city. The stone in course of time became a large tree bearing lovely fruit. The king ordered a fence to be put round the tree, and placed a guard lest people should eat of the fruit and die. There lived in that city an old Brahman and his wife, who used to live upon charity. The Brahman one day mourned his hard lot, and told his wife that instead of leading the wretched life of a beggar he would eat the fruit of the poisonous tree in the king's garden and thus end his days. So that very night he got up from his bed in order to get into the king's garden. His wife, suspecting her husband's intention, followed him, resolved also to eat of the fruit and die with her husband. As at that dead hour of night the guard was asleep, the old Brahman plucked a fruit and ate it. The woman said to her husband, 'If you die what is the use of my life? I'll also eat and die.' So saying she plucked a fruit and ate it. Thinking that the poison would take some time to produce its due effect, they both went home and lay in bed, supposing that they would never rise again. To their infinite surprise next morning they found themselves to be not only alive, but young and vigorous. Their neighbours could scarcely recognise them—they had become so changed. The old Brahman had become handsome and vigorous, no grey hairs, no wrinkles on his cheeks; and as for his wife, she had become as beautiful as any lady in the king's household. The king, hearing of this wonderful change, sent for the old Brahman, who told him all the circumstances. The king then greatly lamented the sad fate of his pet bird, and blamed himself for having killed it without fully inquiring into the case.

"Hence it is," continued the youngest prince, "that I told your majesty that before you cut off a man's head you should inquire whether the man is really guilty. I know your majesty thinks that last night I entered your chamber with wicked intent. Be pleased to hear me before you strike. Last night as I was on my rounds I saw a female figure come out of the palace. On challenging her she said that she was Rajlakshmi, the guardian deity of the palace; and that she was leaving the palace as the king would be killed that night. I told her to come in, and that I would prevent the king from being killed. I went straight into your bedroom, and saw a large cobra going round and round your golden bedstead. I killed the cobra, cut it up into a hundred pieces, and put them in the pan dish. But while I was cutting up the snake, a drop of its blood fell on the breast of my mother; and then I thought that while I had saved my father I had killed my mother. I wrapped round my tongue a piece of cloth sevenfold and licked up the drop of blood. While I was licking up the blood, my mother opened her eyes and noticed me. This is what I have done; now cut off my head if your majesty wishes it."

The king filled with joy and gratitude embraced his son, and from that time loved him more even than he had loved him before.

1. The tutelary goddess of a king's household.
2. A vessel, made generally of brass, for keeping the pan leaf together with betel-nut and other spices.

5

The Adventures of Two Thieves and of their Sons

PART - I

Once upon a time there lived two thieves in a village who earned their livelihood by stealing. As they were well-known thieves, every act of theft in the village was ascribed to them whether they committed it or not; they therefore left the village, and, being resolved to support themselves by honest labour, went to a neighbouring town for service. Both of them were engaged by a householder; the one had to tend a cow, and the other to water a champaka plant. The elder thief began watering the plant early in the morning, and as he had been told to go on pouring water till some of it collected itself round the foot of the plant he went on pouring bucketful after bucketful: but to no purpose. No sooner was the water poured on the foot of the plant than it was forthwith sucked up by the thirsty earth; and it was late in the afternoon when the thief, tired with drawing water, laid himself down on the ground, and fell asleep. The younger thief fared no better. The cow which he had to tend was the most vicious in the whole country. When taken out of the village for pasturage it galloped away to a great distance with its tail erect; it ran from one paddy-field to another, and ate the corn and trod upon it; it entered into sugar-cane plantations and destroyed the sweet cane;—for all which damage and acts of trespass the neat-herd was soundly rated by the owners of the fields. What with running after the cow from field to field, from pool to pool; what with the abusive language poured not only upon him, but upon his forefathers up to the fourteenth generation, by the owners of the fields in which the corn had been destroyed,—the younger thief had a miserable day of it. After a world of trouble he succeeded about sunset in catching hold of the cow, which he brought back to the house of his master. The elder thief had just roused himself from sleep when he saw the younger one bringing in the cow. Then the elder said to the younger—"Brother, why are you so late in coming from the fields?"

Younger. What shall I say, brother? I took the cow to that part of the meadow where there is a tank, near which there is a large tree. I let the cow loose, and it began to graze about without giving the least trouble. I spread my gamchha1 upon the grass under the tree; and there was such a delicious breeze that I soon fell asleep, and I did not wake till after sunset; and when I awoke I saw my good cow grazing contentedly at the distance of a few paces. But how did you fare, brother?

Elder. Oh, as for me, I had a jolly time of it. I had poured only one bucketful of water on the plant, when a large quantity rested round it. So my work was done, and I had the whole day to myself. I laid myself down on the ground; I meditated on the joys of this new mode of life; I whistled; I sang; and at last fell asleep. And I am up only this moment.

When this talk was ended, the elder thief, believing that what the younger thief had said was true, thought that tending the cow was more comfortable than watering the plant; and the younger thief, for the same reason, thought that watering the plant was more comfortable than tending the cow: each therefore resolved to exchange his own work for that of the other.

Elder. Well, brother, I have a wish to tend the cow. Suppose to-morrow you take my work, and I yours. Have you any objection?

Younger. Not the slightest, brother. I shall be glad to take up your work, and you are quite welcome to take up mine. Only let me give you a bit of advice. I felt it rather uncomfortable to sleep nearly the whole of the day on the bare ground. If you take a charpoy2 with you, you will have a merry time of it.

Early the following morning the elder thief went out with the cow to the fields, not forgetting to take with him a charpoy for his ease and comfort; and the younger thief began watering the plant. The latter had thought that one bucketful, or at the outside two bucketfuls, of water would be enough. But what was his surprise when he found that even a hundred bucketfuls were not sufficient to saturate the ground around the roots of the plant. He was dead tired with drawing water. The sun was almost going down, and yet his work was not over. At last he gave it up through sheer weariness.

The elder thief in the fields was in no better case. He took the cow beside the tank which the younger thief had spoken of, put his charpoy under the large tree hard by, and then let the cow loose. As soon as the cow was let loose it went scampering about in the meadow, jumping over hedges and ditches, running through paddy-fields, and injuring sugar-cane plantations. The elder thief was not a little put about. He had to run about the whole day, and to be insulted by the people whose fields had been trespassed upon. But the worst of it was, that our thief had to run about the meadow with the charpoy on his head, for he could not put it anywhere for fear it should be taken away. When the other neat-herds who were in the meadow saw the elder thief running about in breathless haste after the cow with the charpoy on his head, they clapped their hands and raised shouts of derision. The poor fellow, hungry and angry, bitterly repented of the exchange he had made. After infinite trouble, and with the help of the other neat-herds, he at last caught hold of the precious cow, and brought it home long after the village lamps had been lit.

When the two thieves met in the house of their master, they merely laughed at each other without speaking a word. Their dinner over, they laid themselves to rest, when there took place the following conversation:—

Younger. Well, how did you fare, brother?

Elder. Just as you fared, and perhaps some degrees better.

Younger. I am of opinion that our former trade of thieving was infinitely preferable to this sort of honest labour, as people call it.

Elder. What doubt is there of that? But, by the gods, I have never seen a cow which can be compared to this. It has no second in the world in point of viciousness.

Younger. A vicious cow is not a rare thing. I have seen some cows as vicious. But have you ever seen a plant like this champaka plant which you were told to water? I wonder what becomes of all the water that is poured round about it. Is there a tank below its roots?

Elder. I have a good mind to dig round it and see what is beneath it.

Younger. We had better do so this night when the good man of the house and his wife are asleep.

At about midnight the two thieves took spades and shovels and began digging round the plant. After digging a good deal the younger thief lighted upon some hard thing against which the shovel struck. The curiosity of both was excited. The younger thief saw that it was a large jar; he thrust his hand into it and found that it was full of gold mohurs. But he said to the elder thief—"Oh, it is nothing; it is only a large stone." The elder thief, however, suspected that it was something else; but he took care not to give vent to his suspicion. Both agreed to give up digging as they had found nothing; and they went to sleep.

An hour or two after, when the elder thief saw that the younger thief was asleep, he quietly got up and went to the spot which had been digged. He saw the jar filled with gold mohurs. Digging a little near it, he found another jar also filled with gold mohurs. Overjoyed to find the treasure, he resolved to secure it. He took up both the jars, went to the tank which was near, and from which water used to be drawn for the plant, and buried them in the mud of its bank. He then returned to the house, and quietly laid himself down beside the younger thief, who was then fast asleep. The younger thief, who had first found the jar of gold mohurs, now woke, and softly stealing out of bed, went to secure the treasure he had seen. On going to the spot he did not see any jar; he therefore naturally thought that his companion the elder thief had secreted it somewhere. He went to his sleeping partner, with a view to discover if possible by any marks on his body the place where the treasure had been hidden. He examined the person of his friend with the eye of a detective, and saw mud on his feet and near the ankles. He immediately concluded the treasure must have been concealed somewhere in the tank. But in what part of the tank? on which bank? His ingenuity did not forsake him here. He walked round all the four banks of the tank. When he walked round three sides, the frogs on them jumped into the water; but no frogs jumped from the fourth bank. He therefore concluded that the treasure must have been buried on the fourth bank. In a little he found the two jars filled with gold mohurs; he took them up, and going into the cow-house brought out the vicious cow he had tended, and put the two jars on its back. He left the house and started for his native village.

When the elder thief at crow-cawing got up from sleep, he was surprised not to find his companion beside him. He hastened to the tank and found that the jars were not there. He went to the cow-house, and did not see the vicious cow. He immediately concluded the younger thief must have run away with the treasure on the back of the cow. And where could he think of going? He must be going to his native village. No sooner did this process of reasoning pass through his mind than he resolved forthwith to set out and overtake the younger thief. As he passed through the town, he invested all the money he had in a costly pair of shoes covered with gold lace. He walked very fast, avoiding the public road and making short cuts. He descried the younger thief trudging on slowly with his cow. He went before him in the highway about a distance of 200 yards, and threw down on the road one shoe. He walked on another 200 yards and threw the other shoe at a place near which was a large tree; amid the thick leaves of that tree he hid himself. The younger thief coming along the public road saw the first shoe and said to himself—"What a beautiful shoe that is! It is of gold lace. It would have suited me in my present circumstances now that I have got rich. But what shall I do with one shoe?" So he passed on. In a short time he came to the place where the other shoe was lying. The younger thief said within himself—"Ah, here is the other shoe! What a fool I was, that I did not pick up the one I first saw! However it is not too late. I'll tie the cow to yonder tree and go for the other shoe." He tied the cow to the tree, and taking up the second shoe went for the first, lying at a distance of about 200 yards. In the meantime the elder thief got down from the tree, loosened the cow, and drove it towards his native village, avoiding the king's highway. The younger thief on returning to the tree found that the cow was gone. He of course concluded that it could have been done only by the elder thief. He walked as fast as his legs could carry him, and reached his native village long before the elder thief with the cow. He hid himself near the door of the elder thief's house. The moment the elder thief arrived with the cow, the younger thief accosted him, saying—"So you are come safe, brother. Let us go in and divide the money." To this proposal the elder thief readily agreed. In the inner yard of the house the two jars were taken down from the back of the cow; they went to a room, bolted the door, and began dividing. Two mohurs were taken up by the hand, one was put in one place, and the other in another; and they went on doing that till the jars became empty. But last of all one gold mohur remained. The question was—Who was to take it? Both agreed that it should be changed the next morning, and the silver cash equally divided. But with whom was the single mohur to remain? There was not a little wrangling about the matter. After a great deal of yea and nay, it was settled that it should remain with the elder thief, and that next morning it should be changed and equally divided.

*"They ran away in great fear, leaving behind them the money
and jewels"*

At night the elder thief said to his wife and the other women of the house, "Look here, ladies, the younger thief will come to-morrow morning to demand the share of the remaining gold mohur; but I don't mean to give it to him. You do one thing to-morrow. Spread a cloth on the ground in the yard. I will lay myself on the cloth pretending to be dead; and to convince people that I am dead, put a tulasi3 plant near my head. And when you see the younger thief coming to the door, you set up a loud cry and lamentation. Then he will of course go away, and I shall not have to pay his share of the gold mohur." To this proposal the women readily agreed. Accordingly the next day, about noon, the elder thief laid himself down in the yard like a corpse with the sacred basil near his head. When the younger thief was seen coming near the house, the women set up a loud cry, and when he came nearer and nearer, wondering what it all meant, they said, "Oh, where did you both go? What did you bring? What did you do to him? Look, he is dead!" So saying they rent the air with their cries. The younger thief, seeing through the whole, said, "Well, I am sorry my friend and brother is gone. I must now attend to his funeral. You all go away from this place, you are but women. I'll see to it that the remains are well burnt." He brought a quantity of straw and twisted it into a rope, which he fastened to the legs of the deceased man, and began tugging him, saying that he was going to take him to the place of burning. While the elder thief was being dragged through the streets, his body was getting dreadfully scratched and bruised, but he held his peace, being resolved to act his part out, and thus escape giving the share of the gold mohur. The sun had gone down when the younger thief with the corpse reached the place of burning. But as he was making preparations for a funeral pile, he remembered that he had not brought fire with him. If he went for fire leaving the elder thief behind, he would undoubtedly run away. What then was to be done? At last he tied the straw rope to the branch of a tree, and kept the pretended corpse hanging in the air, and he himself climbed into the tree and sat on that branch, keeping tight hold of the rope lest it should break, and the elder thief run away. While they were in this state, a gang of robbers passed by. On seeing the corpse hanging, the head of the gang said, "This raid of ours has begun very auspiciously. Brahmans and Pandits say that if on starting on a journey one sees a corpse, it is a good omen. Well, we have seen a corpse, it is therefore likely that we shall meet with success this night. If we do, I propose one thing: on our return let us first burn this dead body and then return home." All the robbers agreed to this proposal. The robbers then entered into the house of a rich man in the village, put its inmates to the sword, robbed it of all its treasures, and withal managed it so cleverly that not a mouse stirred in the village. As they were successful beyond measure, they resolved on their return to burn the dead body they had seen. When they came to the place of burning they found the corpse hanging as before, for the elder thief had not yet opened his mouth lest he should be obliged to give half of the gold mohur. The thieves dug a hollow in the ground, brought fuel, and laid it upon the hollow. They took down the corpse from the tree, and laid it upon the pile; and as they were going to set it on fire, the corpse gave out an unearthly scream and jumped up. That very moment the younger thief jumped down from the tree with a similar scream. The robbers were frightened beyond measure. They thought that a Dana (evil spirit) had possessed the corpse, and that a ghost jumped down from the tree. They ran away in great fear, leaving behind them the money and the jewels which they had obtained by robbery. The two thieves laughed heartily, took up all the riches of the robbers, went home, and lived merrily for a long time.

Part II

The elder thief and the younger thief had one son each. As they had been so far successful in life by practising the art of thieving, they resolved to train up their sons to the same profession. There was in the village a Professor of the Science of Roguery, who took pupils, and gave them lessons in that difficult science. The two thieves put their sons under this renowned Professor. The son of the elder thief distinguished himself very much, and bade fair to surpass his father in the art of stealing. The lad's cleverness was tested in the following manner. Not far from the Professor's house there lived a poor man in a hut, upon the thatch of which climbed a creeper of the gourd kind. In the middle of the thatch, which was also its topmost part, there was a splendid gourd, which the man and his wife watched day and night. They certainly slept at night, but then the thatch was so old and rickety that if even a mouse went up to it bits of straw and particles of earth used to fall inside the hut, and the man and his wife slept right below the spot where the gourd was; so that it was next to impossible to steal the gourd without the knowledge of its owners. The Professor said to his pupils— for he had many— that any one who stole the gourd without being caught would be pronounced the dux of the school. Our elder thief's son at once accepted the offer. He said he would steal away the gourd if he were allowed the use of three things, namely, a string, a cat, and a knife. The Professor allowed him the use of these three things. Two or three hours after nightfall, the lad, furnished with the three things mentioned above, sat behind the thatch under the eaves, listening to the conversation carried on by the man and his wife lying in bed inside the hut. In a short time the conversation ceased. The lad then concluded that they must both have fallen asleep. He waited half an hour longer, and hearing no sound inside, gently climbed up on the thatch. Chips of straw and particles of earth fell upon the couple sleeping inside. The woman woke up, and rousing her husband said, "Look there, some one is stealing the gourd!" That moment the lad squeezed the throat of the cat, and puss immediately gave out her usual "Mew! mew! mew!" The husband said, "Don't you hear the cat mewing? There is no thief; it is only a cat." The lad in the meantime cut the gourd from the plant with his knife, and tied the string which he had with him to its stalk. But how was he to get down without being discovered and caught, especially as the man and the woman were now awake? The woman was not convinced that it was only a cat; the shaking of the thatch, and the constant falling of bits of straw and particles of dust, made her think that it was a human being that was upon the thatch. She was telling her husband to go out and see whether a man was not there; but he maintained that it was only a cat. While the man and woman were thus disputing with each other, the lad with great force threw down the cat upon the ground, on which the poor animal purred most vociferously; and the man said aloud to his wife, "There it is; you are now convinced that it was only a cat." In the meantime, during the confusion created by the clamour of the cat and the loud talk of the man, the lad quietly came down from the thatch with the gourd tied to the string.

Next morning the lad produced the gourd before his teacher, and described to him and to his admiring comrades the manner in which he had committed the theft. The Professor was in ecstasy, and remarked, "The worthy son of a worthy father." But the elder thief, the father of our hopeful genius, was by no means satisfied that his son was as yet fit to enter the world. He wanted to prove him still further. Addressing his son he said, "My son, if you can do what I tell you, I'll think you fit to enter the world. If you can steal the gold chain of the queen of this country from her neck, and bring it to me, I'll think you fit to enter the world." The gifted son readily agreed to do the daring deed.

The young thief—for so we shall now call the son of the elder thief—made a reconnaissance of the palace in which the king and queen lived. He reconnoitred all the four gates, and all the outer and inner walls as far as he could; and gathered incidentally a good deal of information, from people living in the neighbourhood, regarding the habits of the king and queen, in what part of the palace they slept, what guards there were near the bedchamber, and who, if any, slept in the antechamber. Armed with all this knowledge the young thief fixed upon one dark night for doing the daring deed. He took with him a sword, a hammer and some large nails, and put on very dark clothes. Thus accoutred he went prowling about the Lion gate of the palace. Before the zenana4 could be got at, four doors, including the Lion gate, had to be passed; and each of these doors had a guard of sixteen stalwart men. The same men, however, did not remain all night at their post. As the king had an infinite number of soldiers at his command, the guards at the doors were relieved every hour; so that once every hour at each door there were thirty-two men present, consisting of the relieving party and of the relieved. The young thief chose that particular moment of time for entering each of the four doors. At the time of relief when he saw the Lion gate crowded with thirty-two men, he joined the crowd without being taken notice of; he then spent the hour preceding the next relief in the large open space and garden between two doors; and he could not be taken notice of, as the night as well as his clothes was pitch dark. In a similar manner he passed the second door, the third door, and the fourth door. And now the queen's bedchamber stared him in the face. It was in the third loft; there was a bright light in it; and a low voice was heard as that of a woman saying something in a humdrum manner. The young thief thought that the voice must be the voice of a maid-servant reciting a story, as he had learnt was the custom in the palace every night, for composing the king and queen to sleep. But how to get up into the third loft? The inner doors were all closed, and there were guards everywhere. But the young thief had with him nails and a hammer: why not drive the nails into the wall and climb up by them? True; but the driving of nails into the wall would make a great noise which would rouse the guards, and possibly the king and queen,—at any rate the maid-servant reciting stories would give the alarm. Our erratic genius had considered that matter well before engaging in the work. There is a water-clock in the palace which shows the hours; and at the end of every hour a very large Chinese gong is struck, the sound of which is so loud that it is not only heard all over the palace, but over most part of the city; and the peculiarity of the gong, as of every Chinese gong, was that nearly one minute must elapse after the first stroke before the second stroke could be made, to allow the gong to give out the whole of its sound. The thief fixed upon the minutes when the gong was struck at the end of every hour for driving nails into the wall. At ten o'clock when the gong was struck ten times, the thief found it easy to drive ten nails into the wall. When the gong stopped, the thief also stopped, and either sat or stood quiet on the ninth nail catching hold of the tenth which was above the other. At eleven o'clock he drove into the wall in a similar manner eleven nails, and got a little higher than the second story; and by twelve o'clock he was in the loft where the royal bedchamber was. Peeping in he saw a drowsy maid-servant drowsily reciting a story, and the king and queen apparently asleep. He went stealthily behind the story-telling maid-servant and took his seat. The queen was lying down on a richly furnished bedstead of gold beside the king. The massive chain of gold round the neck of the queen was gleaming in candle-light. The thief quietly listened to the story of the drowsy maid-servant. She was becoming more and more sleepy. She stopped for a second, nodded her head, and again resumed the story. It was plain she was under the influence of sleep. In a moment the thief cut off the head of the maid-servant with his sword, and himself went on reciting for some minutes the story which the woman was telling. The king and queen were unconscious of any change as to the person of the story-teller, for they were both in deep sleep. He stripped the murdered woman of her clothes, put them on himself, tied up his own clothes in a bundle, and walking softly, gently took off the chain from the neck of the queen. He then went through the rooms down stairs, ordered the inner guard to open the door, as she was obliged to go out of the palace for purposes of necessity. The guards, seeing that it was the queen's maid-servant, readily allowed her to go out. In the same manner, and with the same pretext, he got through the other doors, and at last out into the street. That very night, or rather morning, the young thief put into his father's hand the gold chain of the queen. The elder thief could scarcely believe his own eyes. It was so like a dream. His joy knew no bounds. Addressing his son he said—"Well done, my son; you are not only as clever as your father, but you have beaten me hollow. The gods give you long life, my son."

Next morning when the king and queen got up from bed, they were shocked to see the maid-servant lying in a pool of blood. The queen also found that her gold chain was not round her neck. They could not make out how all this could have taken place. How could any thief manage to elude the vigilance of so many guards? How could he get into the queen's bedchamber? And how could he again escape? The king found from the reports of the guards that a person calling herself the royal maid-servant had gone out of the palace some hours before dawn. All sorts of inquiries were made, but in vain. Proclamation was made in the city; a large reward was offered to any one who would give information tending to the apprehension of the thief and murderer. But no one responded to the call. At last the king ordered a camel to be brought to him. On the back of the animal was placed two large bags filled with gold mohurs. The man taking charge of the bags upon the camel was ordered to go through every part of the city making the following challenge:—"As the thief was daring enough to steal away a gold chain from the neck of the queen, let him further show his daring by stealing the gold mohurs from the back of this camel." Two days and nights the camel paraded through the city, but nothing happened. On the third night as the camel-driver was going his rounds he was accosted by a sannyasi,5 who sat on a tiger's skin before a fire, and near whom was a monstrous pair of tongs. This sannyasi was no other than the young thief in disguise. The sannyasi said to the camel-driver— "Brother, why are you going through the city in this manner? Who is there so daring as to steal from the back of the king's camel? Come down, friend, and smoke with me." The camel-driver alighted, tied the camel to a tree on the spot, and began smoking. The mendicant supplied him not only with tobacco, but with ganja and other intoxicating drugs, so that in a short time the camel-driver became quite intoxicated and fell asleep. The young thief led away the camel with the treasure on its back in the dead of night, through narrow lanes and bye-paths to his own house. That very night the camel was killed, and its carcase buried in deep pits in the earth, and the thing was so managed that no one could discover any trace of it.

The next morning when the king heard that the camel-driver was lying drunk in the street, and that the camel had been made away with together with the treasure, he was almost beside himself with anger. Proclamation was made in the city to the effect that whoever caught the thief would get the reward of a lakh of rupees. The son of the younger thief—who, by the way, was in the same school of roguery with the son of the elder thief, though he did not distinguish himself so much—now came to the front and said that he would apprehend the thief.

He of course suspected that the son of the elder thief must have done it—for who so daring and clever as he? In the evening of the following day the son of the younger thief disguised himself as a woman, and coming to that part of the town where the young thief lived, began to weep very much, and went from door to door saying—

"The camel-driver alighted, tied the camel to a tree on the spot, and began smoking"

"O sirs, can any of you give me a bit of camel's flesh, for my son is dying, and the doctors say nothing but eating camel's meat can save his life. O for pity's sake, do give me a bit of camel's flesh." At last he went to the house of the young thief, and begged of the wife—for the young thief himself was out—to tell him where he could get hold of camel's flesh, as his son would assuredly perish if it could not be got. Saying this he rent the air with his cries, and fell down at the feet of the young thief's wife. Woman as she was, though the wife of a thief, she felt pity for the supposed woman, and said—"Wait, and I will try and get some camel's flesh for your son." So saying, she secretly went to the spot where the dead camel had been buried, brought a small quantity of flesh, and gave it to the party. The son of the younger thief was now entranced with joy. He went and told the king that he had succeeded in tracing the thief, and would be ready to deliver him up at night if the king would send some constables with him. At night the elder thief and his son were captured, the body of the camel dug out, and all the treasures in the house seized. The following morning the king sat in judgment. The son of the elder thief confessed that he had stolen the queen's gold chain, and killed the maid-servant, and had taken away the camel; but he added that the person who had detected him and his father—the younger thief—were also thieves and murderers, of which fact he gave undoubted proofs. As the king had promised to give a lakh of rupees to the detective, that sum was placed before the son of the younger thief. But soon after he ordered four pits to be dug in the earth in which were buried alive, with all sorts of thorns and thistles, the elder thief and the younger thief, and their two sons.

1. A towel used in bathing.
2. A sort of bed made of rope, supported by posts of wood.
3. The sacred basil.
4. Zenana is not the name of a province in India, as the good people of Scotland the other day took it to be, but the innermost department of a Hindu or Mohammedan house which the women occupy.
5. A religious mendicant.

6

The Ghost-Brahman

Once on a time there lived a poor Brahman, who not being a Kulin, found it the hardest thing in the world to get married. He went to rich people and begged of them to give him money that he might marry a wife. And a large sum of money was needed, not so much for the expenses of the wedding, as for giving to the parents of the bride. He begged from door to door, flattered many rich folk, and at last succeeded in scraping together the sum needed. The wedding took place in due time; and he brought home his wife to his mother. After a short time he said to his mother—"Mother, I have no means to support you and my wife; I must therefore go to distant countries to get money somehow or other. I may be away for years, for I won't return till I get a good sum. In the meantime I'll give you what I have; you make the best of it, and take care of my wife." The Brahman receiving his mother's blessing set out on his travels. In the evening of that very day, a ghost assuming the exact appearance of the Brahman came into the house. The newly married woman, thinking it was her husband, said to him—"How is it that you have returned so soon? You said you might be away for years; why have you changed your mind?" The ghost said—"To-day is not a lucky day, I have therefore returned home; besides, I have already got some money." The mother did not doubt but that it was her son. So the ghost lived in the house as if he was its owner, and as if he was the son of the old woman and the husband of the young woman. As the ghost and the Brahman were exactly like each other in everything, like two peas, the people in the neighbourhood all thought that the ghost was the real Brahman. After some years the Brahman returned from his travels; and what was his surprise when he found another like him in the house. The ghost said to the Brahman—"Who are you? what business have you to come to my house?" "Who am I?" replied the Brahman, "let me ask who you are. This is my house; that is my mother, and this is my wife." The ghost said—"Why herein is a strange thing. Every one knows that this is my house, that is my wife, and yonder is my mother; and I have lived here for years. And you pretend this is your house, and that woman is your wife. Your head must have got turned, Brahman." So saying the ghost drove away the Brahman from his house. The Brahman became mute with wonder. He did not know what to do. At last he bethought himself of going to the king and of laying his case before him. The king saw the ghost-Brahman as well as the Brahman, and the one was the picture of the other; so he was in a fix, and did not know how to decide the quarrel. Day after day the Brahman went to the king and besought him to give him back his house, his wife, and his mother; and the king, not knowing what to say every time, put him off to the following day. Every day the king tells him to—"Come to-morrow"; and every day the Brahman goes away from the palace weeping and striking his forehead with the palm of his hand, and saying—"What a wicked world this is! I am driven from my own house, and another fellow has taken possession of my house and of my wife! And what a king this is! He does not do justice."

"'How is it that you have returned so soon?'"

Now, it came to pass that as the Brahman went away every day from the court outside the town, he passed a spot at which a great many cowboys used to play. They let the cows graze on the meadow, while they themselves met together under a large tree to play. And they played at royalty. One cowboy was elected king; another, prime minister or vizier; another, kotwal, or prefect of the police; and others, constables. Every day for several days together they saw the Brahman passing by weeping. One day the cowboy king asked his vizier whether he knew why the Brahman wept every day. On the vizier not being able to answer the question, the cowboy king ordered one of his constables to bring the Brahman to him. One of them went and said to the Brahman—"The king requires your immediate attendance." The Brahman replied—"What for? I have just come from the king, and he put me off till to-morrow. Why does he want me again?" "It is our king that wants you— our neat-herd king," rejoined the constable. "Who is neat-herd king?" asked the Brahman. "Come and see," was the reply. The neat-herd king then asked the Brahman why he every day went away weeping. The Brahman then told him his sad story. The neat-herd king, after hearing the whole, said, "I understand your case; I will give you again all your rights. Only go to the king and ask his permission for me to decide your case." The Brahman went back to the king of the country, and begged his Majesty to send his case to the neat-herd king, who had offered to decide it. The king, whom the case had greatly puzzled, granted the permission sought. The following morning was fixed for the trial. The neat-herd king, who saw through the whole, brought with him next day a phial with a narrow neck. The Brahman and the ghost-Brahman both appeared at the bar. After a great deal of examination of witnesses and of speech-making, the neat-herd king said—"Well, I have heard enough. I'll decide the case at once. Here is this phial. Whichever of you will enter into it shall be declared by the court to be the rightful owner of the house the title of which is in dispute. Now, let me see, which of you will enter." The Brahman said—"You are a neat-herd, and your intellect is that of a neat-herd. What man can enter into such a small phial?" "If you cannot enter," said the neat-herd king, "then you are not the rightful owner. What do you say, sir, to this?" turning to the ghost-Brahman and addressing him. "If you can enter into the phial, then the house and the wife and the mother become yours." "Of course I will enter," said the ghost. And true to his word, to the wonder of all, he made himself into a small creature like an insect, and entered into the phial. The neat-herd king forthwith corked up the phial, and the ghost could not get out. Then, addressing the Brahman, the neat-herd king said, "Throw this phial into the bottom of the sea, and take possession of your house, wife, and mother." The Brahman did so, and lived happily for many years and begat sons and daughters.

7

The Man who wished to be Perfect

Once on a time a religious mendicant came to a king who had no issue, and said to him, "As you are anxious to have a son, I can give to the queen a drug, by swallowing which she will give birth to twin sons; but I will give the medicine on this condition, that of those twins you will give one to me, and keep the other yourself." The king thought the condition somewhat hard, but as he was anxious to have a son to bear his name, and inherit his wealth and kingdom, he at last agreed to the terms. Accordingly the queen swallowed the drug, and in due time gave birth to two sons. The twin brothers became one year old, two years old, three years old, four years old, five years old, and still the mendicant did not appear to claim his share; the king and queen therefore thought that the mendicant, who was old, was dead, and dismissed all fears from their minds. But the mendicant was not dead, but living; he was counting the years carefully. The young princes were put under tutors, and made rapid progress in learning, as well as in the arts of riding and shooting with the bow; and as they were uncommonly handsome, they were admired by all the people. When the princes were sixteen years old the mendicant made his appearance at the palace gate, and demanded the fulfilment of the king's promise. The hearts of the king and of the queen were dried up within them. They had thought that the mendicant was no more in the land of the living; but what was their surprise when they saw him standing at the gate in flesh and blood, and demanding one of the young princes for himself? The king and queen were plunged into a sea of grief. There was nothing for it, however, but to part with one of the princes; for the mendicant might by his curse turn into ashes not only both the princes, but also the king, queen, palace, and the whole of the kingdom to boot. But which one was to be given away? The one was as dear as the other. A fearful struggle arose in the hearts of the king and queen. As for the young princes, each of them said, "I'll go," "I'll go." The younger one said to the elder, "You are older, if only by a few minutes; you are the pride of my father; you remain at home, I'll go with the mendicant." The elder said to the younger, "You are younger than I am; you are the joy of my mother; you remain at home, I'll go with the mendicant." After a great deal of yea and nay, after a great deal of mourning and lamentation, after the queen had wetted her clothes with her tears, the elder prince was let go with the mendicant. But before the prince left his father's roof he planted with his own hands a tree in the courtyard of the palace, and said to his parents and brother, "This tree is my life. When you see the tree green and fresh, then know that it is well with me; when you see the tree fade in some parts, then know that I am in an ill case; and when you see the whole tree fade, then know that I am dead and gone." Then kissing and embracing the king and queen and his brother, he followed the mendicant.

As the mendicant and the prince were wending their way towards the forest they saw some dog's whelps on the roadside. One of the whelps said to its dam, "Mother, I wish to go with that handsome young man, who must be a prince." The dam said, "Go"; and the prince gladly took the puppy as his companion. They had not gone far when upon a tree on the roadside they saw a hawk and its young ones. One of the young ones said to its dam, "Mother, I wish to go with that handsome young man, who must be the son of a king." The hawk said, "Go"; and the prince gladly took the young hawk as his companion. So the mendicant, the prince, with the puppy and the young hawk, went on their journey. At last they went into the depth of the forest far away from the houses of men, where they stopped before a hut thatched with leaves. That was the mendicant's cell. The mendicant said to the prince, "You are to live in this hut with me. Your chief work will be to cull flowers from the forest for my devotions. You can go on every side except the north. If you go towards the north evil will betide you. You can eat whatever fruit or root you like; and for your drink, you will get it from the brook." The prince disliked neither the place nor his work. At dawn he used to cull flowers in the forest and give them to the mendicant; after which the mendicant went away somewhere the whole day and did not return till sundown; so the prince had the whole day to himself. He used to walk about in the forest with his two companions—the puppy and the young hawk. He used to shoot arrows at the deer, of which there was a great number; and thus made the best of his time. One day as he pierced a stag with an arrow, the wounded stag ran towards the north, and the prince, not thinking of the mendicant's behest, followed the stag, which entered into a fine-looking house that stood close by. The prince entered, but instead of finding the deer he saw a young woman of matchless beauty sitting near the door with a dice-table set before her. The prince was rooted to the spot while he admired the heaven-born beauty of the lady. "Come in, stranger," said the lady; "chance has brought you here, but don't go away without having with me a game of dice." The prince gladly agreed to the proposal. As it was a game of risk they agreed that if the prince lost the game he should give his young hawk to the lady; and that if the lady lost it, she should give to the prince a young hawk just like that of the prince. The lady won the game; she therefore took the prince's young hawk and kept it in a hole covered with a plank.

"At dawn he used to cull flowers in the forest"

The prince offered to play a second time, and the lady agreeing to it, they fell to it again, on the condition that if the lady won the game she should take the prince's puppy, and if she lost it she should give to the prince a puppy just like that of the prince. The lady won again, and stowed away the puppy in another hole with a plank upon it. The prince offered to play a third time, and the wager was that, if the prince lost the game, he should give himself up to the lady to be done to by her anything she pleased; and that if he won, the lady should give him a young man exactly like himself. The lady won the game a third time; she therefore caught hold of the prince and put him in a hole covered over with a plank. Now, the beautiful lady was not a woman at all; she was a Rakshasi who lived upon human flesh, and her mouth watered at the sight of the tender body of the young prince. But as she had had her food that day she reserved the prince for the meal of the following day.

Meantime there was great weeping in the house of the prince's father. His brother used every day to look at the tree planted in the courtyard by his own hand. Hitherto he had found the leaves of a living green colour; but suddenly he found some leaves fading. He gave the alarm to the king and queen, and told them how the leaves were fading. They concluded that the life of the elder prince must be in great danger. The younger prince therefore resolved to go to the help of his brother, but before going he planted a tree in the courtyard of the palace, similar to the one his brother had planted, and which was to be the index of the manner of his life. He chose the swiftest steed in the king's stables, and galloped towards the forest. In the way he saw a dog with a puppy, and the puppy thinking that the rider was the same that had taken away his fellow-cub—for the two princes were exactly like each other—said, "As you have taken away my brother, take me also with you." The younger prince understanding that his brother had taken away a puppy, he took up that cub as a companion. Further on, a young hawk, which was perched on a tree on the roadside, said to the prince, "You have taken away my brother; take me also, I beseech you"; on which the younger prince readily took it up. With these companions he went into the heart of the forest, where he saw a hut which he supposed to be the mendicant's. But neither the mendicant nor his brother was there. Not knowing what to do or where to go, he dismounted from his horse, allowed it to graze, while he himself sat inside the house. At sunset the mendicant returned to his hut, and seeing the younger prince, said, "I am glad to see you. I told your brother never to go towards the north, for evil in that case would betide him; but it seems that, disobeying my orders, he has gone to the north and has fallen into the toils of a Rakshasi who lives there. There is no hope of rescuing him; perhaps he has already been devoured." The younger prince forthwith went towards the north, where he saw a stag which he pierced with an arrow. The stag ran into a house which stood by, and the younger prince followed it. He was not a little astonished when, instead of seeing a stag, he saw a woman of exquisite beauty. He immediately concluded, from what he had heard from the mendicant, that the pretended woman was none other than the Rakshasi in whose power his brother was. The lady asked him to play a game of dice with her. He complied with the request, and on the same conditions on which the elder prince had played. The younger prince won; on which the lady produced the young hawk from the hole and gave it to the prince. The joy of the two hawks on meeting each other was great. The lady and the prince played a second time, and the prince won again. The lady therefore brought to the prince the young puppy lying in the hole. They played a third time, and the prince won a third time. The lady demurred to producing a young man exactly like the prince, pretending that it was impossible to get one; but on the prince insisting upon the fulfilment of the condition, his brother was produced. The joy of the two brothers on meeting each other was great. The Rakshasi said to the princes, "Don't kill me, and I will tell you a secret which will save the life of the elder prince." She then told them that the mendicant was a worshipper of the goddess Kali, who had a temple not far off; that he belonged to that sect of Hindus who seek perfection from intercourse with the spirits of departed men; that he had already sacrificed at the altar of Kali six human victims whose skulls could be seen in niches inside her temple; that he would become perfect when the seventh victim was sacrificed; and that the elder prince was intended for the seventh victim. The Rakshasi then told the prince to go immediately to the temple to find out the truth of what she had said. To the temple they accordingly went. When the elder prince went inside the temple, the skulls in the niches laughed a ghastly laugh. Horror-struck at the sight and sound, he inquired the cause of the laughter; and the skulls told him that they were glad because they were about to get another added to their number. One of the skulls, as spokesman of the rest, said, "Young prince, in a few days the mendicant's devotions will be completed, and you will be brought into this temple and your head will be cut off, and you will keep company with us. But there is one way by which you can escape that fate and do us good." "Oh, do tell me," said the prince, "what that way is, and I promise to do you all the good I can." The skull replied, "When the mendicant brings you into this temple to offer you up as a sacrifice, before cutting off your head he will tell you to prostrate yourself before Mother Kali, and while you prostrate yourself he will cut off your head. But take our advice, when he tells you to bow down before Kali, you tell him that as a prince you never bowed down to any one, that you never knew what bowing down was, and that the mendicant should show it to you by himself doing it in your presence. And when he bows down to show you how it is done, you take up your sword and separate his head from his body. And when you do that we shall all be restored to life, as the mendicant's vows will be unfulfilled." The elder prince thanked the skulls for their advice, and went into the hut of the mendicant along with his younger brother.

In the course of a few days the mendicant's devotions were completed. On the following day he told the prince to go along with him to the temple of Kali, for what reason he did not mention; but the prince knew it was to offer him up as a victim to the goddess. The younger prince also went with them, but he was not allowed to go inside the temple. The mendicant then stood in the presence of Kali and said to the prince, "Bow down to the goddess." The prince replied, "I have not, as a prince, bowed to any one; I do not know how to perform the act of prostration. Please show me the way first, and I'll gladly do it." The mendicant then prostrated himself before the goddess; and while he was doing so the prince at one stroke of his sword separated his head from his body. Immediately the skulls in the niches of the temple laughed aloud, and the goddess herself became propitious to the prince and gave him that virtue of perfection which the mendicant had sought to obtain. The skulls were again united to their respective bodies and became living men, and the two princes returned to their country.

8

A Ghostly Wife

Once on a time there lived a Brahman who had married a wife, and who lived in the same house with his mother. Near his house was a tank, on the embankment of which stood a tree, on the boughs of which lived a ghost of the kind called Sankchinni.1 One night the Brahman's wife had occasion to go to the tank, and as she went she brushed by a Sankchinni who stood near; on which the she-ghost got very angry with the woman, seized her by the throat, climbed into her tree, and thrust her into a hole in the trunk. There the woman lay almost dead with fear. The ghost put on the clothes of the woman and went into the house of the Brahman. Neither the Brahman nor his mother had any inkling of the change. The Brahman thought his wife returned from the tank, and the mother thought that it was her daughter-in-law. Next morning the mother-in-law discovered some change in her daughter-in-law. Her daughter-in-law, she knew, was constitutionally weak and languid, and took a long time to do the work of the house. But she had apparently become quite a different person. All of a sudden she had become very active. She now did the work of the house in an incredibly short time. Suspecting nothing, the old woman said nothing either to her son or to her daughter-in-law; on the contrary, she inly rejoiced that her daughter-in-law had turned over a new leaf. But her surprise became every day greater and greater. The cooking of the household was done in much less time than before. When the mother-in-law wanted the daughter-in-law to bring anything from the next room, it was brought in much less time than was required in walking from one room to the other. The ghost, instead of going inside the next room, would stretch a long arm—for ghosts can lengthen or shorten any limb of their bodies—from the door and get the thing. One day the old woman observed the ghost doing this. She ordered her to bring a vessel from some distance, and the ghost unconsciously stretched her hand to several yards' distance, and brought it in a trice. The old woman was struck with wonder at the sight. She said nothing to her, but spoke to her son. Both mother and son began to watch the ghost more narrowly. One day the old woman knew that there was no fire in the house, and she knew also that her daughter-in-law had not gone out of doors to get it; and yet, strange to say, the hearth in the kitchen-room was quite in a blaze. She went in, and, to her infinite surprise, found that her daughter-in-law was not using any fuel for cooking, but had thrust into the oven her foot, which was blazing brightly. The old mother told her son what she had seen, and they both concluded that the young woman in the house was not his real wife but a she-ghost. The son witnessed those very acts of the ghost which his mother had seen. An Ojha2 was therefore sent for. The exorcist came, and wanted in the first instance to ascertain whether the woman was a real woman or a ghost. For this purpose he lighted a piece of turmeric and set it below the nose of the supposed woman. Now this was an infallible test, as no ghost, whether male or female, can put up with the smell of burnt turmeric. The moment the lighted turmeric was taken near her, she screamed aloud and ran away from the room. It was now plain that she was either a ghost or a woman possessed by a ghost. The woman was caught hold of by main force and asked who she was. At first she refused to make any disclosures, on which the Ojha took up his slippers and began belabouring her with them. Then the ghost said with a strong nasal accent—for all ghosts speak through the nose— that she was a Sankchinni, that she lived on a tree by the side of the tank, that she had seized the young Brahmani and put her in the hollow of her tree because one night she had touched her, and that if any person went to the hole the woman would be found. The woman was brought from the tree almost dead; the ghost was again shoebeaten, after which process, on her declaring solemnly that she would not again do any harm to the Brahman and his family, she was released from the spell of the Ojha and sent away; and the wife of the Brahman recovered slowly. After which the Brahman and his wife lived many years happily together and begat many sons and daughters.

1. Sankchinnis or Sankhachurnis are female ghosts of white complexion. They usually stand at the dead of night at the foot of trees, and look like sheets of white cloth.
2. An exorcist, one who drives away ghosts from possessed persons.

9

The Story of a Brahmadaitya[1]

Once on a time there lived a poor Brahman who had a wife. As he had no means of livelihood, he used every day to beg from door to door, and thus got some rice which they boiled and ate, together with some greens which they gleaned from the fields. After some time it chanced that the village changed its owner, and the Brahman bethought himself of asking some boon of the new laird. So one morning the Brahman went to the laird's house to pay him court. It so happened that at that time the laird was making inquiries of his servants about the village and its various parts. The laird was told that a certain banyan-tree in the outskirts of the village was haunted by a number of ghosts; and that no man had ever the boldness to go to that tree at night. In bygone days some rash fellows went to the tree at night, but the necks of them all were wrung, and they all died. Since that time no man had ventured to go to the tree at night, though in the day some neat-herds took their cows to the spot. The new laird on hearing this said, that if any one would go at night to the tree, cut one of its branches and bring it to him, he would make him a present of a hundred bighas[2] of rent-free land.

"*The moment the first stroke was given, a great many ghosts rushed towards the Brahman*"

None of the servants of the laird accepted the challenge, as they were sure they would be throttled by the ghosts. The Brahman, who was sitting there, thought within himself thus—"I am almost starved to death now, as I never get my bellyful. If I go to the tree at night and succeed in cutting off one of its branches I shall get one hundred bighas of rent-free land, and become independent for life. If the ghosts kill me, my case will not be worse, for to die of hunger is no better than to be killed by ghosts." He then offered to go to the tree and cut off a branch that night. The laird renewed his promise, and said to the Brahman that if he succeeded in bringing one of the branches of that haunted tree at night he would certainly give him one hundred bighas of rent-free land.

In the course of the day when the people of the village heard of the laird's promise and of the Brahman's offer, they all pitied the poor man. They blamed him for his foolhardiness, as they were sure the ghosts would kill him, as they had killed so many before. His wife tried to dissuade him from the rash undertaking; but in vain. He said he would die in any case; but there was some chance of his escaping, and of thus becoming independent for life. Accordingly, one hour after sundown, the Brahman set out. He went to the outskirts of the village without the slightest fear as far as a certain vakula-tree (Mimusops Elengi), from which the haunted tree was about one rope distant. But under the vakula-tree the Brahman's heart misgave him. He began to quake with fear, and the heaving of his heart was like the upward and downward motion of the paddy-husking pedal. The vakula-tree was the haunt of a Brahmadaitya, who, seeing the Brahman stop under the tree, spoke to him, and said, "Are you afraid, Brahman? Tell me what you wish to do, and I'll help you. I am a Brahmadaitya." The Brahman replied, "O blessed spirit, I wish to go to yonder banyan-tree, and cut off one of its branches for the zemindar, who has promised to give me one hundred bighas of rent-free land for it. But my courage is failing me. I shall thank you very much for helping me." The Brahmadaitya answered, "Certainly I'll help you, Brahman. Go on towards the tree, and I'll come with you." The Brahman, relying on the supernatural strength of his invisible patron, who is the object of the fear and reverence of common ghosts, fearlessly walked towards the haunted tree, on reaching which he began to cut a branch with the bill which was in his hand. But the moment the first stroke was given, a great many ghosts rushed towards the Brahman, who would have been torn to pieces but for the interference of the Brahmadaitya. The Brahmadaitya said in a commanding tone, "Ghosts, listen. This is a poor Brahman. He wishes to get a branch of this tree which will be of great use to him. It is my will that you let him cut a branch." The ghosts, hearing the voice of the Brahmadaitya, replied, "Be it according to thy will, lord. At thy bidding we are ready to do anything. Let not the Brahman take the trouble of cutting; we ourselves will cut a branch for him." So saying, in the twinkling of an eye, the ghosts put into the hands of the Brahman a branch of the tree, with which he went as fast as his legs could carry him to the house of the zemindar. The zemindar and his people were not a little surprised to see the branch; but he said, "Well, I must see to-morrow whether this branch is a branch of the haunted tree or not; if it be, you will get the promised reward."

Next morning the zemindar himself went along with his servants to the haunted tree, and found to their infinite surprise that the branch in their hands was really a branch of that tree, as they saw the part from which it had been cut off. Being thus satisfied, the zemindar ordered a deed to be drawn up, by which he gave to the Brahman for ever one hundred bighas of rent-free land. Thus in one night the Brahman became a rich man.

It so happened that the fields, of which the Brahman became the owner, were covered with ripe paddy, ready for the sickle. But the Brahman had not the means to reap the golden harvest. He had not a pice in his pocket for paying the wages of the reapers. What was the Brahman to do? He went to his spirit-friend the Brahmadaitya, and said, "Oh, Brahmadaitya, I am in great distress. Through your kindness I got the rent-free land all covered with ripe paddy. But I have not the means of cutting the paddy, as I am a poor man. What shall I do?" The kind Brahmadaitya answered, "Oh, Brahman, don't be troubled in your mind about the matter. I'll see to it that the paddy is not only cut, but that the corn is threshed and stored up in granaries, and the straw piled up in ricks. Only you do one thing. Borrow from men in the village one hundred sickles, and put them all at the foot of this tree at night. Prepare also the exact spot on which the grain and the straw are to be stored up."

The joy of the Brahman knew no bounds. He easily got a hundred sickles, as the husbandmen of the village, knowing that he had become rich, readily lent him what he wanted. At sunset he took the hundred sickles and put them beneath the vakula-tree. He also selected a spot of ground near his hut for his magazine of paddy and for his ricks of straw; and washed the spot with a solution of cow-dung and water. After making these preparations he went to sleep.

In the meantime, soon after nightfall, when the villagers had all retired to their houses, the Brahmadaitya called to him the ghosts of the haunted tree, who were one hundred in number, and said to them, "You must to-night do some work for the poor Brahman whom I am befriending. The hundred bighas of land which he has got from the zemindar are all covered with standing ripe corn. He has not the means to reap it. This night you all must do the work for him. Here are, you see, a hundred sickles; let each of you take a sickle in hand and come to the field I shall show him. There are a hundred of you. Let each ghost cut the paddy of one bigha, bring the sheaves on his back to the Brahman's house, thresh the corn, put the corn in one large granary, and pile up the straw in separate ricks. Now, don't lose time. You must do it all this very night." The hundred ghosts at once said to the Brahmadaitya, "We are ready to do whatever your lordship commands us." The Brahmadaitya showed the ghosts the Brahman's house, and the spot prepared for receiving the grain and the straw, and then took them to the Brahman's fields, all waving with the golden harvest. The ghosts at once fell to it. A ghost harvest-reaper is different from a human harvest-reaper. What a man cuts in a whole day, a ghost cuts in a minute. Mash, mash, mash, the sickles went round, and the long stalks of paddy fell to the ground. The reaping over, the ghosts took up the sheaves on their huge backs and carried them all to the Brahman's house. The ghosts then separated the grain from the straw, stored up the grain in one huge store-house, and piled up the straw in many a fantastic rick. It was full two hours before sunrise when the ghosts finished their work and retired to rest on their tree. No words can tell either the joy of the Brahman and his wife when early next morning they opened the door of their hut, or the surprise of the villagers, when they saw the huge granary and the fantastic ricks of straw. The villagers did not understand it. They at once ascribed it to the gods.

A few days after this the Brahman went to the vakula-tree and said to the Brahmadaitya, "I have one more favour to ask of you, Brahmadaitya. As the gods have been very gracious to me, I wish to feed one thousand Brahmans; and I shall thank you for providing me with the materials of the feast." "With the greatest pleasure," said the polite Brahmadaitya; "I'll supply you with the requirements of a feast for a thousand Brahmans; only show me the cellars in which the provisions are to be stored away." The Brahman improvised a store-room. The day before the feast the store-room was overflowing with provisions. There were one hundred jars of ghi (clarified butter), one hill of flour, one hundred jars of sugar, one hundred jars of milk, curds, and congealed milk, and the other thousand and one things required in a great Brahmanical feast. The next morning one hundred Brahman pastrycooks were employed; the thousand Brahmans ate their fill; but the host, the Brahman of the story, did not eat. He thought he would eat with the Brahmadaitya. But the Brahmadaitya, who was present there though unseen, told him that he could not gratify him on that point, as by befriending the Brahman the Brahmadaitya's allotted period had come to an end, and the pushpaka[3] chariot had been sent to him from heaven. The Brahmadaitya, being released from his ghostly life, was taken up into heaven; and the Brahman lived happily for many years, begetting sons and grandsons.

1. The ghost of a Brahman who dies unmarried.
2. A bigha is about the third part of an acre.
3. The chariot of Kuvera, the Hindu god of riches.

www.ingramcontent.com/pod-product-compliance
Lightning Source LLC
Chambersburg PA
CBHW051759130726
47987CB00003B/1023